The Thing Is

Short Stories of Things &
the People They Encounter

The Thing Is

*Short Stories of Things &
the People They Encounter*

Written & Illustrated by

Rivers Houseal

NOGGINNOSE
PRESS

The Thing Is

ISBN 978-1-956611-03-8

Illustrations by Rivers Houseal
Cover design and content layout by Houseal Creative
Edited by Rachel Nix

Nogginnose Press
PO Box 96
Smithville, AR 72466 USA
nogginnose.com

*To Mumsie, who is the reason
I wrote three of these stories, and
had faith in me even when I told her
one of them would be about a potato.*

*Also, to Robbie. We never met,
but your typewriter inspired (and
typed) my favorite of these stories.
Your wordsmithing blood flows in
my veins. I wish we could have
bantered about books together over
foaming cups of tea—but this will
have to do, this side of Heaven.*

Contents

Of When a
Typewriter Was Found

and the Events That Followed

I n my part of the world, at least, to see a typewriter sitting in the middle of the road is not normal. But if I have learned one thing, it is that odd things do happen, and there it sat. Furthermore, I was raised to know that when one spies a typewriter in trouble, one rescues it. So I did.

Once the typewriter was safe, I realized that my parents had let me down. They had failed to teach me what one is supposed to do with a rescued typewriter. I supposed the only natural thing to do was to try to find the owner, and I further supposed that the only way to do that was to post an advertisement in the newspaper. So I did.

FOUND

Smith-Corona 'Silent' Typewriter
Found on Old Coast Road, halfway
between Portlethen and Downies.
Misses its owner terribly.

CONTACT

Emma MacMorrel
Portlethen Village, Aberdeen, AB12

Weeks passed, and nothing came of it. I believe that typewriter was beginning to think of me as its mother. It was becoming a fixture in my old roll-top. Both the newspaper office clerk and the telegram boy got tired of my asking if anything had come up, and both assured me that the typewriter's owners obviously were not inclined or not able to reclaim it, and that I might consider myself the rightful owner of a new Smith-Corona typewriter.

So, for the first time, I sat down, and I typed at it. Just a little bit. When I began, I had not the smoke of a notion what I was getting myself into. I began by typing my name. After that, I didn't know what to do, so I typed another name…a made-up one. I supposed that meant I had made a person. What does one do with a made-up person after she is made? To just leave her name there on my paper with nothing else seemed awfully rude of me, so I made her do something. To be precise, I made her bake a pie.

Then, it occurred to me how very silly it would be for a woman to bake a pie for herself to be eaten all alone. (I then remembered that I did this all the time. Nevertheless, for my made-up person, it was silly.) So I made a friend for her. And then a third being, to offer some more variety of conversation. Along came a fourth, for no good reason, then a fifth, a sixth, and so on and so forth until poor Claudia (the first one) had quite a house full, and was practically begging for me to un-create some of these people so she could have some peace and quiet.

I was beginning to tire of them all too; managing thirteen or some-odd lives is exhausting. It seemed ill-mannered of me to have fashioned all these characters only to kill them all off (though I know authors who have done it), so I simply sent them all home with my best wishes. For those who needed prompting, I just made up some pressing family obligations for them, and off they went.

At last, Claudia had her quiet, and the two of us settled in for a nice chat. Now, to be her maker, I found myself surprised at how very little I knew about her. I sensed that this young woman might have some wonderful stories to tell me, so I brewed myself a cup—all right; a *pot*—of Earl Grey, and typed one out for her as well.

Come to find out, she was a masterful seamstress, read voraciously, nearly killed herself making sauerkraut last year, and hadn't a living relative in the world. At this, I felt a kinship with Claudia. I begged her to go on. Well, she told me, she had just completed a cathedral window quilt that had plagued her for years, but was too afraid to display it on the guest room bed lest it be *sat on*. Her prize-winning pig had run away the night before—that was the reason for the black ribbon hung upon her front door. This last explanation was a relief to me; I had been worrying that one of the surplus characters had up and died, after all.

Following this divulgence, Claudia turned to look at me with those soft brown eyes—no wait,

I changed my mind, they're blue—and asked for me to tell her about myself. Myself! Now this was an odd thing. Fictional characters do not typically inquire after their author. I was taken aback.

I looked away from the typewriter for a moment and considered my dusky parlor. I was all alone…conversing with my fictional people as if they really sat before me. Perhaps I was going 'round the bend, after all.

I decided, if I was, there was no one but Claudia around to know anyway. So I indulged her, and I told her my story.

I told her of what life was like for a child in the poorer section of Glasgow. Of how other children thought having a birthmark shaped like a bunny on the back of one's neck was a hilarious thing, and of how I often wished it were shaped like a wolf, instead, and that it could come to life and scare them all off their mocking laughter. Claudia cried with me when I described the long nights of tears and nightmares after losing my father to the vices of a Glasgow street gang. I told her of my mother's hands, cut, calloused, and blue from long days of factory labor, and of my joy at seeing them grow warm and hale after she was able to move us to a small town on the coast.

Though I'd had a rough start, I told Claudia, our move to the country marked for me the start of a very happy spell of life, and one of prosperity for me and my mother, until my mother's death in a milking accident and my subsequent trip to a boarding school. Claudia was horrified—until I reassured her that the school I was blessed to be sent to was relatively warm in heart and hearth, and was only my home for two years before I was able to claim my mother's thatch cottage on the coast again.

Claudia was delighted to hear that the five years following had been pleasant ones, even if they were spent alone. My cares had been only trivial. She inquired after my life as it was now, and my prospects, and I told her of my enterprise as the keeper of the village bookshop in Portlethen, and of my small spot of land and its charms. I confided that though I was happy enough alone, if a fellow ever did show up to take my hand, I was afraid I would say something foolish, like "Finally!"

She laughed at that, and told me she found herself in the same way. I began to think I had made a sister for myself.

She asked how I spent my evenings on my farm. I was quick to correct her that it was not a proper farm, quite, but that I did have a large bed of flowers and a pig, both of which required care each evening after my return from Portlethen.

Claudia thrilled to hear this, exclaiming that flower gardens were her foible—another surprise to me—and that she preferred lavender over thyme for cooking, and which did I prefer? I told her I would have to disagree and choose thyme, but that my favorites to grow were dog roses and chamomile.

I told Claudia just how very worried I was that my pig was developing influenza. She offered me condolences on my almost certain loss, having only just lost a pig herself. After that brief excursion, there was a moment of silence, and we decided to move on to cleaner topics, such as the proper way to launder a white-worked handkerchief.

It was at this moment that I yawned, and I began to think perhaps I had better leave Claudia and see about some supper. My paper companion was still feeling talkative, and I realized that if I let her have her way, I would have no supper for a while yet. So—do *not* tell her—I made her yawn, too.

My supper fixed up quickly, and when one lives alone, there are hardly any dirty dishes to speak of. So it was not long before I found myself curious again to see what Claudia was up to. When I returned to the typewriter to see, I found her disgruntled—with me!

Let me tell you, it is a strange thing for one's own characters to be mad at one, but as I am sure other authors would verify, it does happen, and one has only to make the best of it. The ungrateful little things do come around, eventually.

Perhaps I need to take this moment to assure any straggling readers who may yet be hanging on with me, that I am *not* crazy. If it seems strange to you that I talk to my characters like real people and react to their emotions as if I had nothing to do with the creation of them, then you obviously have never dreamt up a character on the fly, just for the fun of it.

Book folk who are figured up over time, in character sketches and illustrations, and who undergo great deliberations from their maker over what their name should be, are generally more put together, more refined in their knowledge of life, and more familiar with the normal behavior of a book character than one who is invented on the spot and told to get going. Such spontaneous characters must, of necessity, have a mind of their own.

A hastily made character is born knowing more about herself than her author knows. Such characters are great fun, as I hope my runabout with Claudia will already have shown, but they can be great trials in that they have no comprehension of how the author-character relationship is supposed to run. They are supposed to be docile, obedient, and preferably unaware that they are being controlled; but a hastily made character is rarely told this, so they are not docile, they are not obedient, and by one means and another they end up knowing far too much about their author for anyone's good.

There now; I am not crazy. It may now be necessary to prove to my patient reader that I am not—at least—confused. (Baby steps, baby steps.) Lest I lose any remaining readers I may still have, let us get back to Claudia.

To my embarrassment, I learned that Claudia had got wise to the fact that I wrote up some sleepiness for her just for the sake of my stomach, and she was offended. Though I gave my best efforts to an apology, she remained miffed. It occurred to me that my little Claudia was, after all, a woman. So I typed the following...

```
Chocolate cake.
```

It didn't make the situation *all* better, but it did improve it to no small degree. She still wanted to know why I put her away, but she was in a more obliging mood to be receiving my excuses.

I explained to her, as tactfully as I could, that I enjoyed our time together as much as she did, but that unlike her, I could not just have someone type food into existence for me anytime the need arose. (Whoops! I had let slip the fact that she was dependent on me…anyway, it didn't seem to register in her mind; I was yet safe.) As for *my* sustenance, I had to do the arranging myself. It really did not take me long, and she didn't know how blessed she was, I pointed out. I might have had a family to cook for, and wash for, and generally care for, and then think how long she would have to wait! Humbled, she conceded that she had been selfish. I thought she had suffered enough and forwent my lecture on the proper subservience of a fictional character.

We talked on, across a range of—as things happened—entirely unrelated subjects. Soon, I began to feel uneasy about my time on the typewriter. Sure, I had begun with no plan, but wasn't a writer supposed to write something meaningful? I made sure to think my thoughts where Claudia could not hear them, lest I hurt her feelings a second time...but I wondered if perhaps I had wasted an afternoon in creating this friend who did nothing except sit in her old-fashioned parlor and listen to me go on about myself. When was Claudia going to get up and do something? She needed a purpose—an answer for her existence. She needed to tell a story. I began to regret rushing headlong into a tale. (An adventure, rather; Claudia must never know she is not real. It would hurt her pride royally.)

There were only two things I could do.

One, I could start from scratch. I could pull out the typing paper I was working on and tuck it on a shelf as a memento of an afternoon blissfully spent, and I could roll up a fresh sheet and start again when I had some sort of plan for forging ahead into a fresh story.

Two, I could try to redeem the story I had already begun. This was my first whack at writing anything...other than synopses of theology works, in school. I reckoned that if I actually went somewhere with the story, I could only end up with something that sounded awfully amateur and ill-thought-out. Which would be what it was...but I would not want anyone to *know* that.

My head began to hurt. My conscience was in turmoil. Abandon my first labor of love and potentially create something worth my while, or persevere (by which I meant stubbornly plugging along, without aim, despite all reasonable arguments against the idea)?

I looked at my page and at where I had left Claudia. She was stirring yet another lump of sugar into her tea, and the breeze danced through the lace curtains over her open parlor window and into her hair. She looked at me and smiled.

I knew I could not leave her. After all, what better use had I for the next few months' worth of evenings? I determined that I would do it: I would make something of Claudia, and if I possibly could, it would be something good.

I think my sudden burst of resolve may have frightened Claudia a smidgen, but she turned her full attention on me when I announced that we needed to talk. I explained how I felt she needed some purpose, some work, some... some...someone to make pies for. She seemed interested.

We starting by making a list of her friends, and discussing who should be the first recipient. I helped her draw up a roster: this week, I said she should bring a pie to dear Widow

Kierney, and Claudia said yes, and it ought to be a mincemeat. All right, said I, very well. Next week, it would be Matthew Davies and his young wife Lisa, and we agreed their little boy Evan would appreciate apple pie. Week following, Mr. and Mrs. Horton Thusby would get a chicken pie; and so on and so forth until poor Claudia found herself busy for three months coming, and I began to worry that she would need another purpose…a fallback, if you will.

I had lit the fire in Claudia's belly by now, and she went off to fetch her apron and set to on the first pie. She left me alone with her parlor. I began to think, and I thinked up another purpose for her—but I kept it to myself. I added another name in the middle of the pie-delivery schedule: Johnny Ruthven. I added his name again three weeks later, and I hoped Claudia would not notice how often Johnny would be getting a pie from her. I added him to the roster just once more, two weeks after the last time, and then I sat back to watch the chips fall.

What a silly notion, I then thought—the idea of the writer of a story sitting back as if things will come to pass at their own will, with no help from the Instigator.

There are times when an author has no plan (as we have established, I did not), and so to end up with a story they simply jump into a rabbit-hole and see where they fall out. When they find their feet, they jump into another hole, then another, and so on until maybe they find that their jumping had some rhythmic order to it, and their story had a subconscious plan, after all. At least, so I had heard. I had just jumped into a very mysterious rabbit-hole, and I was still waiting to see where I would fall out.

Flash ahead a few weeks, and I was accompanying Claudia to the residence of Mr. Ruthven. Other than declaring his existence, I had heretofore given no further thought to him, so I thought frantically about him while I walked with Claudia so that we might have something besides a name to greet us. Claudia was in a conversational mood that day, as it happened, so to give myself time to think, I made her stop and admire the view of the glen. That worked, but not for long, so I decided she would have to be poetic.

While she stood staring at the horizon for nearly half an hour trying to find a rhyme for "beauteous", I sat down in the road and pondered Johnny Ruthven. He would be tall, but not very.

Brown hair. No—red. He would be a Scot through and through. A beard? No. He would be a sheep farmer, and have a sheepdog named Knox. There; that was sufficient for now. Wait! He would have to like rabbit pie, as that was the particular variety Claudia carried—and was about to drop, *goodness gracious!* I saved the pie from imminent splatting, snapped my Claudia-come-poetess from her reverie, and we carried on.

Perhaps my reader is suspicious of my intentions on adding a young bachelor to Claudia's pie registry. Well, speculate and whisper no more: it is true. I intended to marry Claudia off.

It did not take long for my contrivances to bear fruit—with me pulling the strings, it was not hard. Before long, I had the two of them talking over Claudia's pies and laughing over some book or another. Things continued to escalate, and almost before I had caught on, they had me planning their wedding.

My word! Planning a book wedding is excruciating. Every detail, every word of the ceremony, every word the guests said, every morsel of food that got eaten (never mind the washing up), all responsibility rested on the shoulders of Yours truly. Only now did I start to wonder if I should have left well enough alone. But Claudia was so happy. So I put on a smile and got that wedding together without any of the real-life benefits of delegation.

Oh, but then—surprise and horror— Claudia asked me to be the flower girl. I tell you, I did not know whether to be honored, mortified, or scared that she had again begun doing things I am fairly certain I never told her to do. However it happened, come wedding day, I traipsed down the aisle of her Norman village church and cast rose petals delicately onto the rug. Only to have them stomped into that same rug by merry wedding-goers a little later. (It was all right though, I learned. Fictional rugs are easily cleaned.)

That wedding exhausted me, and as soon as I sent Johnny and Claudia down the road in that '35 automobile of his, I pushed away from my writing desk with every intention of giving them over to a three-week honeymoon, and myself to a three-week break. I went to bed, and it was a long time before I sat at my roll-top again.

Eventually, I began to feel a strange longing to see Claudia again. So I sat down at my desk. I slowly removed the cloth I had thrown over my foundling typewriter to keep the dust off, and I looked to see what had become of that dear girl.

She was very happy to see me, but I found her much more busied than I had left her. She took to married life like lavender to shortbread, and it suited her well. By and by, behold! a very small Ruthven came to join them, and I found my Claudia busier than ever. She no longer had the liberty to sit in the parlor and while away an afternoon in light conversation, and I saw clearer than anything that my approach in putting down her life story on paper was going to have to change.

Now, one must not forget that I had a job to attend to at the bookshop in Portlethen. It kept me there from nine in the morning till five in the afternoon, thereby leaving me only my evenings to visit with Claudia. So, one morning shortly after this, I uprooted my typewriter from the desk at home and lugged it with me to work, where between the in and out of Portlethen and Downies folk in search of reading material, I acted on my new strategy of finding out about Claudia.

Which was: to observe her at her wifely work. As I watched her (*made* her; I keep forgetting I was in charge) care for her husband and baby,

I became keenly aware that I had succeeded in finding a good, satisfactory purpose for her. My ramblings became focused on chronicling her motherhood, and I loved every moment of it. The keys of my typewriter hammered like never before. I am afraid the folk of Portlethen must have worried about me, distracted as I was about everything else.

The stack of pages that were filled with Claudia's gleanings and observances grew to be quite tall, and I no longer felt I needed to keep making excuses for the unplanned nature of my story. It, like Claudia, had found a purpose, and one so enrapturing that it made me wish I could experience what Claudia did, here in my home of Real Life.

Now that I did my work in a public place, people began to hear about what I was up to and to offer me encouragement. I think some of them came into the bookshop solely for that purpose. Many of them expressed a desire to read my work when it was through, and I was in utter wonder at the idea. Of course, a writer who begins as I did daydreams about the *possibility* of being read, but she does not *expect* to be read. So when it happens, or when it starts to look like it might happen, she is in awe.

Claudia's middle grew as my book did, and soon enough she had two small Ruthvens running about the place. Her Johnny grew that beard, after all. Such small things became the crowning thrills of my working days. I never knew such joy as I did in the writing of her *purpose*. What a sublime word!

Then came the glorious day when I stood up from my desk chair, stretched my back, and gazed down at a stack of papers a hand-breadth tall. I was done. The thought of it seemed so strange; Claudia had always been such a real, living thing to me. But the day had come when I just knew—Claudia and her little family were ready to meet the world and teach it the lesson they had taught me: that not all which seems directionless really is. There is a guiding Hand that holds it, beyond view, and just a bit longer, and purpose may appear out of nowhere. I was done, and I was infinitely happy.

Then came a yet more wondrous day... the day when I held a letter from an honored publishing firm in Inverness informing me that *The Chronicles of Claudia Ruthven* had been accepted for publication. I lived for a while in a state of shock—a glorious, awed shock. I wondered often about Claudia and her dear ones, and I wondered how I would find her if I were to go looking for her in her world again. I did go visit her from time to time.

But I think the wonder to top all wonders came when I held a hard copy in my hands for the first time. I think I cried; I don't remember. To experience that is to see all the hopes, fears, joys, and cups of Earl Grey that go into writing a story manifested into something you can recognize as wonderful. And the feeling does not pass with time. Perhaps that is the best thing about it.

Why, I feel it now, as I look at that hardcover volume sitting on my desk, reminding me and all who see it of what can happen to you when you find a typewriter sitting in the middle of the road.

The Paternal
Time-Keeper

It was not yet opening hours, so as usual, I had to let myself in. That tarnished old doorbell, original to the late-Victorian shop structure, announced my perfectly-timed arrival to work at Runnels' Clock & Repair. However, the sleepy darkness of the front room told me there was nobody around to hear about it.

I thought it was odd that Mr. Runnels was not yet at work, but no matter. I knew my way about as well as the Runnels family did. My mood dampened as my exposed fingers and nose reminded me that his lateness meant the shop was not really warmer than the outdoors, after all, but I was not going to have any depression setting in. I whistled the chorus of "Loch Lomond" to keep my thoughts cheery (and my cheeks warm) as I headed to the back to rouse the furnace for its day's work. A diligent furnace it is, and within minutes I shed my coat.

I was standing halfway in the coat closet, busy arranging my coat, scarf, and cap in their respective places when the door from the front room opened suddenly with an ill-tempered groan. It harmonized well with the mutterings its opener was giving off.

I turned and smiled. "Amelia! Good morning."

Miss Amelia Runnels stood with her gloves in her hand. She stared at the back wall contemplatively. "Hmm. Yes. Good morning, Evelyn. No family to leave you in the lurch; I suppose it *is* a good morning, isn't it?"

I blinked and looked away. Well then. That jab was callous, uncalled-for, and it had sting—and I was not immune. It was also uncharacteristic. I had never heard of Amelia Runnels being praised for her tact, but this was not the foot on which our mornings usually started.

Yet, aloud, I only noticed the problem she implied concerning the family that she *did* have. "Did something happen? I was surprised not to see your father. He's usually here and has half of a clock built before I arrive."

Amelia sighed deeply. "Yes. But not this morning, Evelyn. As you see."

I nodded. I waited. Amelia offered nothing more. Disappointed in myself that I could be so weak to curiosity, I gave the line a little tug. "Why not? He's not sick, is he?"

Amelia sighed again. "No, he is not. But it's Sunday—Father is taking off the 'Sabbath', as he called it. He intends to make a habit of it, actually."

I was truly surprised. "Since when?" I exclaimed.

"That? Only this week. I might have seen it coming, but…" I waited for the sigh. It came. "It all happened so suddenly."

I turned away and started sorting the atrocious pile of cogs and coils on the worktable. I was losing patience with Amelia's evasive replies. Anyway, I thought, it was really not my business to press the matter any more. If she wanted to tell me her troubles, she would. Amelia and I grew up together, working in this shop. She might not be my favorite conversation partner, but she was in some measure my friend, and I hers. She would vent if she wanted to. Meanwhile, I had work to do.

She sat down opposite me and likewise began working furiously on the pile of spare parts. She worked so fast and so heedlessly that several times she almost sent my lovely stacks of balance wheels into the floor. I bit my tongue and hoped that she would either go find something else to do, or blurt whatever was steaming inside of her before her boiler exploded. After bending over for the third time to pick up a clock part from the floor, I almost prompted more conversation to help things along. But no, no; it was none of my business—if she wanted to tell me, she would.

Apparently she did. Finally, something gave, and her pent-up frustrations hit me full in the face. "They have taken up with a group—Father and Mother have, that is." Amelia swept aside the clock parts she had been sorting. I caught one cog as it dropped off the edge of the table. "Mother spends a whole hour in her room every morning, *poring* over that book—"

"What book?" I interrupted. I hated to, but it seemed obvious now that she wanted to tell me what was afoot. I was afraid that nothing she said would make sense unless I was clear about this book that was causing trouble.

"Her Bible," Amelia said, scowling as if I ought to know. "Mother *pores* over it, and will not come down to breakfast until she has 'satisfied her hunger', as she says. What that's all about, I don't know. Refusing to take breakfast until you have *satisfied your hunger?* What sort of sense does that make? Anyway, when she finally *does* come down, she is so...well, *meditative* that she is no good for conversation for another half-hour. Father has started a habit of waking at a quarter to five, so that he has time to get in as much *Bible* as he can before he comes to the shop."

I have always enjoyed literature, and I tend to see everything in life as events in a storyline. Amelia Runnels' story seemed to be failing to build on an important aspect of its plot. I stopped untangling watch coils and attempted to clarify. "You say this situation is a *problem?*"

Amelia looked at me with equal the patience of a misunderstood toddler. "Yes!"

I was still thinking in terms of analyzing a story plot, so my Shakespeare showed itself: "Pray...why?"

Amelia sputtered three random syllables and apparently decided I was too dimwitted today to be of much sympathy. She left me and went off to fervidly fold dust cloths—which had been perfectly folded until she touched them.

But Amelia needed someone with whom to commiserate this morning; that was clear. "Yes, Evelyn! It *is* a problem. They are totally absorbed in this 'new life,'" she resumed. "Mother adores the very *smell* of the *leather* of her Bible. She reveres that book as if it's guarding some secret that it only reveals to those who neglect their lives and become slaves to it. If that is the case, upon my word, it ought to be revealed to her shortly! Now Father has decided to cut out all Sundays' work from our revenue. He and mother are sitting in church as we speak. I could barely convince him to allow you and I to come in today. As it is, we are only allowed to tidy up the shop—no business at all. We are *strictly* ordered."

I thought she might have just revealed some of the problem. Both the young Runnels were fully grown-up, but I could see how it would be a trial to anyone, child or otherwise, to be routinely ignored every morning. I cautiously probed here. "Surely they don't neglect you and your brother, with all this going on?"

"Oh, no." (So much for that theory.) "But Herbert is certainly no help with all of it."

"Is he interested in the 'group' as well?" I am not sure Amelia appreciated my teasing her word choice. In any case, she ignored it.

"Yes. He has *succumbed*." Her bombastic italics throughout this conversation were funny enough to be laughed at, but I did not think it would be in my best interest to do that. Amelia continued. "Herbert does show a little more sense than our parents, but it is *unnerving* to see him so pensive whenever Father or Mother quotes a line from that conniving book which they claim 'spoke to them.' Are they in so deep they are *hearing things?*"

I did not reply this time. I had gotten pretty thoughtful, myself. I had never heard a word about religion from the Runnels, in all my years with them. From Amelia, I had actually heard a few scornful remarks about this or that local church—delicately expressed, of course. *There* must be the real issue, I decided. She saw this situation as if she were losing her parents to their obsession with a new hobby, and that "hobby" happened to be something she considered ridiculous.

Amelia interpreted my silence as disregard for her troubles. She did not say anything more to me for a few minutes. However, like me, she could not deny her curiosity for long. She cocked her head and studied me. "Evelyn…incidentally, where would a debate find you?"

"A debate? What do you mean?"

"Well, you know—about Christianity and such. What are your beliefs?"

"I prefer to stay out of debates entirely." I smiled innocently, as I usually did by way of a polite answer whenever anyone asked me that sort of question. "It is my experience that those who take a stern stand one way or the other come to disappointing places, one way or another."

Amelia raised an eyebrow interestedly. "I suppose they would call you an *agnostic*, then, wouldn't they?"

"I don't know what that means, so I wouldn't take notice if they did."

We sat through a few minutes of productive silence before Amelia tossed a limp rag into my lap. "Well, Evelyn, I believe we need some coffee to warm us. Suppose we leave off dusting religion, and you start dusting the Paternal Time-Keeper?"

I agreed to that as a wonderful idea.

My habit is to swipe at light switches when I turn them on. It is an incautious and, as my grandmother warned me back during my childhood, an "appallingly unladylike" way to turn on the lights. But the one place I am relieved of this bad habit is when I enter the showroom of Mr. Runnels' clock shop. Then, I stop to flip the switch methodically, because in doing so I am illuminating a hallowed place.

One has to maneuver carefully to avoid knocking knees with some piece of furniture there, but everything that takes up floor space in the showroom is a treasure to me. The walls are lined with oak shelves, full of every kind of timepiece known to the English world. Directly in front of the door—truly, only about two small paces away—is the glass counter and showcase, with the freshly painted register perched in a dignified place, turned at just the right dignified angle. There is a small, old-fashioned shop window on either side of the door. In one of these is a brass hat stand cut off short, from which dangle half-a-dozen gold, silver, and brass pocket watches. In the opposite window, a child passing by outside might stop to be fascinated by two fancifully carved cuckoo clocks.

But my favorite nook, by far, has always been the one that houses the Paternal Time-Keeper. It is the only longcase clock in the shop, and the only clock that is never, ever, to be sold.

This particular eighteenth-century grand-father clock holds a place of honor with everyone at Runnels' Clock & Repair. Mr. Runnels was the first to balk at such a common name for such an uncommon beauty, and he declared very shortly after its advent in the shop that it should be referred to as the Paternal Time-Keeper rather than the undignified title of 'grandfather clock.' The younger pair of Runnels and I were expected to keep the Paternal Time-Keeper entirely dust-free, but Mr. Runnels would suffer no one but himself to care for the inner workings of the fatherly wooden presence.

On this Sunday morning, I hummed softly as I set to chasing the dust from the twist carvings under the clock face.

Click!

I shrieked and jumped back in shock as something hard and fast suddenly struck my left cheek. It took me a moment to recover. Wincing, I put a cool finger on the welt now crowning my left cheekbone—I could not tell, to be sure, but I was fairly certain it would be red. Or mottled black and blue. Or, judging by the malicious throb pulsing through it, it might even be a combination of all three colors. I glanced around for something that might have done the hurting, but every solitary article in the immaculate showroom was exactly where it should be. I scowled at the thought of a bird loose in the shop and turned my attention back to the—

Clock face! The round glass door protecting the face of the Paternal Time-Keeper stood wide open, brandishing the protruding brass latch on the outward edge of its frame. The latch was exactly level with my growing welt. Well, at least now it was known why I might be scarred for life. I was perfectly certain that my hands had been nowhere near the release mechanism of the door latch when it flew open. Why there would be such a powerful spring in there to fling it open in such a reckless manner *anyway*, I certainly did not know.

I reached up to close the door, and pushed on the latch to engage it. But the receiving bit flatly refused to receive. In the back of my mind, I was considering what might happen if I were unable to fix the stubborn latch. Most likely, Mr. and Mrs. Runnels would hold my long and unblemished service record as proof that I had not been tampering with the Paternal Time Keeper inappropriately. But still…this clock was Mr. Runnels' darling.

I swatted a wisp of hair from my vision and brandished Mr. Runnels' repair tweezers. After a brief investigation of the latch-works, I found a little point of paper sticking out of a gap. I am no expert on clockworks, but I was fairly certain *that* was not right.

I grasped the paper point with the tweezers and gave a little tug. More paper came into view. It came and came until it showed itself to be a wedge too big to come through easily—but I would have none of that. Another firm tug and I stood blinking at the cream-colored folded triangle in my palm.

I reached up and tried again to shut the door of the clock face. The latch engaged with an obedient *click*. The Paternal Time-Keeper stared back at me with an innocence that was perfectly shocking. I ignored it and unfolded the paper: it was only about three inches square, and remarkably yellow and thin, but it held together well enough to unfold without a rip. The paper bore a bit of writing, which surprised me—though I could not have told what else I might have expected to find there. I read:

You know, my God,
When I lay down to repose;
You determine the hour of my rising.
Shall man stand with God
At the helm of Time's ship
And presume to direct its sailing?
The Psalmist of old placed
His Times in Thine hands;
To be wise, I must do the same.
For an hour shan't pass 'til
You bid it, "Be done"—
Thine hands deal each minute to each need.

I knew very well that I did not understand this poem, but some part of me felt keenly that these words were the hiding place of some beauty. I knew I desperately *wanted* to understand.

The clearing of a feminine throat made me look up. Amelia stood in the doorway. Whatever three parts authority mixed with two parts curiosity look like, the same was all over her face. She was trying to understand what she had just walked in on.

Amelia was my age, and a fellow employee in this shop; but she also happened to be the shop owner's daughter. Our friendship was such that even on ordinary days I was never far from remembering that she could, in fact, pull rank on me whenever she liked. And just now, it crossed my mind that this might look odd—me holding an obviously old piece of paper and standing rather too close to the Paternal Time-Keeper.

I held out the paper for her to take. Amelia flashed me a curious look as she took it. She scanned the writing without comment.

"Pretty, isn't it?" I prompted, after an awkward half-minute.

Amelia looked at me pityingly. "Really, Evelyn. I thought better of you. Such poor rhyme and rubbish subject matter hardly make for a thing of beauty." I wanted to challenge her deeming it "rubbish subject matter," but I had not a whiff of an idea how to go about doing that.

"Where did this come from?" she wanted to know.

I had only the truth to tell, and on its own, that truth was not damning. Who knew; to someone else, the truth might sound logical enough. *Here goes*, I thought. There went. "It was behind the latch of the Paternal Time-Keeper's face...door...thingummy." *So much for sounding logical...*

Amelia's lips pressed into a thin, purple line (strangely reminiscent of a vein in marble).

I looked her in the eyes and watched our ranks grow a little further apart. "How did you come to know that, Evelyn?" she asked, quietly.

I took a deep breath. "A very interesting set of events led to that discovery, all of which I feel your father should know about. You have my word, Amelia, I shall be sure to tell him first thing tomorrow morning."

I excused myself and left to find the coffee before Amelia could have a chance to re-inflate.

—

A half hour before it was time to open the shop next morning, I made my confession to Mr. Runnels. While he studied the tiny yellow parchment with wide eyes, I fingered the edge of the glass counter and felt like a defendant waiting for a jury to come back from lunch and tell me what they thought of me.

After a minute, Mr. Runnels handed the paper to his wife for examination. While she did so, he stepped over to the Paternal Time-Keeper and began eagerly inspecting the door and latch-works. I could not tell if the color on his cheeks was fascination and excitement at my discovery, or the wrath of an Englishman, politely veiled.

I leaned to get a better view of the side of his face. I decided it would be safe to offer a defense. "I promise, sir, I was not at all trying to tamper with the Paternal Time-Keeper. It... rather made me."

Mr. Runnels turned back with a tiny start, as if he had forgotten I was still waiting for judgement. Then, wonder of all, he smiled so widely that his pince-nez slid down on his nose. He began to chuckle—then to laugh uproariously.

"It rather made you—it would certainly seem that way, my dear!" he concurred, his cheeks full of mirth. This decidedly eased the nervousness I was doing my best to hide.

Amelia's brother, Herbert, took his turn studying my find. He flipped the paper over and over in his hands, examining each crease and hand-written figure with wonder. "Father, how long do you suppose this has been in the Paternal Time-Keeper?"

"Only God could know. It is very old, I would think—see the odd way the author makes his S? When I bought the Paternal Time-Keeper, the previous owner assured me that it was a very special clock, with a lesson to teach a wise and willing ear. Long have I tried to be that ear, but behold! It opens for Evelyn!"

"It opened rather violently," I muttered, putting cool fingers on my swollen cheekbone and sending Mr. Runnels into another bout of laughter.

Mrs. Runnels wanted another turn admiring the piece of parchment. "Do you suppose the previous owner knew about this, then? Perhaps he even put it there himself."

Mr. Runnels scrunched his nose under his spectacles, causing them to slide down again. "Perhaps, but I am inclined to think it is older than he was, by far. I think whoever built the clock put it there, and put the strong spring in the door-works so that when the paper fell, it would quickly make itself known. I always wondered why that spring was in there. I considered taking it out the last time I tuned up the Paternal Time-Keeper. Oh, how glad I am now that I didn't!"

Herbert Jr. reverently smoothed the paper flat on the glass counter. "But how on earth was that little wedge of paper heavy enough to fall and disengage the door-latch?"

"It comes to my mind that it could be plenty heavy enough with the Lord's orchestrating finger to weight it," Mrs. Runnels observed thoughtfully.

Mr. Runnels smiled tenderly. "Beautifully put, my dear."

Amelia had seated herself across the tiny showroom in one of the window recesses. She had for some minutes been looking quite out of her element. Now she turned on her mother. "Supposing one did not believe that such an 'orchestrating finger' existed. How then would you explain this?"

Mr. Runnels gently raised an eyebrow. "Are you saying that you *can't* find another explanation, my dear?"

Miss Amelia looked extremely uncomfortable. She did not attempt an answer.

Mr. Runnels turned to his son. "Herbert, in answer to your question, I haven't the smallest explanation for how this could have happened— and I do not care." He winked at Herbert and I and smiled, looking at us good-naturedly over his glasses. *Twentieth-century rationalism be scorned*, the look told us. *Be willing to accept a bit of wonder, of a morning.* I was satisfied. I think Herbert was, too.

I chewed on my lip in order to screw up the courage to ask the question that had shadowed my thoughts all night. "What do they mean, sir?"

"Hmm?"

"The beautiful words. What are they talking about?"

"Well, I am still learning, Evelyn, but I think they mean *trust*."

"In what?"

"Well, child, do they not say, just there?"

"Oh. I…I'm perhaps a little afraid to place that trust, I suppose."

Mrs. Runnels smiled brightly. "So was I, dear. And it's not a once-and-done thing, either. Your trust must be placed in God's hands every day, every minute. Oh, how easy it is to give it and then snatch it right back."

Mr. Runnels jabbed a finger at the paper on the counter and shook his head. "We heard those words, or the same meaning, every year of our lives. Did we not, my dear?" he remarked to his wife. Then he faced me and leaned in with a quiet, excited whisper. "But they meant nothing to me until it was *time* for me to hear. And Mrs. Runnels is right: it is all too easy to forget to place that trust. It took much trust for me to cut out a whole day of business, but you see what has come of it: the discovery of this treasure! I think that is my favorite bit, there: *For an hour shan't pass 'til You bid it, 'Be done'—Thine hands deal each minute to each need.*"

Amelia quitted the room. A moment later we heard the back door open and shut. Mr. Runnels sighed. "And it takes much trust to believe that the God who knew *my* Times knows and controls those of my poor daughter as well."

Herbert muttered something to himself. Mrs. Runnels looked up at him. "What was that, son?"

Herbert smiled. "I was just thinking: one Paternal Time-Keeper has turned us to Another."

I considered this. "So the paper has been hidden there for a century or more. Why *now* has it fallen and revealed itself?"

Mr. Runnels smiled and shrugged. "The Paternal Time-Keeper decided it was time."

THE THING IS

Such Precious
Potatoes as These

I had seen trillions of them, and yet this one stood out to me, capturing my attention in all its dusty brown glory. I picked it up.

There was nothing unusual in that; it was what the dozen other young women around me were doing, and what I had been doing for almost a week now. I had heard people call us "land girls"—picking up potatoes and turning our ankles on hidden rocks in the potato field was simply what we did. So you will believe me when I say that I felt like I had seen trillions of potatoes in the last few days alone, and that there was absolutely no reason why this one should catch my attention.

But it did, and for a few moments I stood still and turned it over and over in my hands, taking in each eye, and wrinkle, and the general ugliness of it. Then I noticed that the farmer and his tractor-drawn disk had progressed well ahead of me. The group with pails and burlap sacks plodded steadily along behind him, and I was falling to the rear—and that would not do. I stuffed my potato into my sack and hurried to cover ground, picking up three potatoes the others had missed and working my way back to the front of the troops.

Several of the girls cast curious or amused or possibly concerned glances in my direction as I passed them. Apparently I had been observed at my potato-ey ruminations. I felt very silly. Why on earth would I have been interested in a potato that had a soft spot, an unnatural number of eyes, and had almost been shorn in two by that rusty old disk?

Perhaps I had just been in the sun too long. Yes, that was it. Potatoes must be harvested on a sunny day, to allow them to dry properly before being stored. But the preferences of the human digging them up are rarely taken into consideration, I have noticed. There was not too much heat to mind, for the summer had already begun to cool off, but when one sees nothing but sunny glare combined with endless stretches of damp dirt clods and the sweaty plaid back of the farmer for hours on end, the whole effect can dizzy the brain.

No matter—another hundred yards of field to cover and then the farmer would send us to wash up. He has done exactly the same thing every day I had been here, six days a week. He would rein in the tired old tractor and we would straighten our backs and wait for him to give the signal. He never did so before he had removed his straw hat, untied the handkerchief from around his neck, and given his brow a good mopping. He would inhale deeply, and then (usually) exhale. Then he would wave us in the general direction of the house, and we would all hoist high our sacks, pails, shoes, and what-have-you and make for the pump spigot like we had never known cleanliness. The way we descended on it was, I am sure, amusing—to someone who has never dug potatoes. You have not known dirty until you have dug potatoes.

Normally, there were not so many of us from the Women's Land Army on Mr. Spittle's farm. (Before I continue…I was concerned, as you are, but he does not spit. Ever. Or drool.) Mr. Spittle was one of the main providers of potatoes for his region, and his neighbor was the same for barley; so, naturally, both farmers farmed hefty quantities of their speciality. They had undertaken an agreement, earlier in the harvest, to share us. When time came to bring in the barley, all of us that the government had sent to help Mr. Spittle would march to Mr. Podge's land (his first name is not Hodge—I checked) and bind barley sheaves for a few days. Come time to uproot tubers, Mr. Podge's land girls would come to *our* aid. So it was just now: five extra girls to be lodging in the barn loft, and it was my turn to help Mrs. Spittle cook for them.

This was no drudgery; I always looked forward to my name being one of the two drawn from Marianne's hat for "commissary duty," as she thrilled to call it. At 23, Marianne was the oldest member of the WLA on Mr. Spittle's farm, and she ruled the roost when Mr. or Mrs. Spittle were not around. Funny…her name was never drawn for commissary duty.

Tonight, it was to be Ruth and me. This made me happy; Ruth is a charming person to cook with. Lighthearted, personable, and a voice like a canary. But the absolute *best* thing about working in the kitchen with Ruth was that she *loves* to wash dishes.

Mrs. Spittle was dear, but more somber than Ruth in the kitchen. This may have been due to the view. She always minded the stove (I presume to keep it out of our inexperienced hands), and on the wall behind it she had hung three pictures: one of each of her sons. One evening, I was watching her gaze at them when she surprised me by turning and giving me a small smile.

"One in France, one in Japan, and one in Africa. I always wanted to travel the world," she told me, "and now I won't have to. They will have done it for me, and they can tell me all about it."

It was barely a week after this when I noticed that she had hung the military tags of one of her sons from his picture. She turned to me again, but this time there was no smile.

"One of them did tell me about it, you see," she almost whispered. "He told me it's so grand in France that he's going to stay there forever." I had failed to notice it before, but I saw now that she had pinned a black ribbon on her dress collar. Later, I saw that Mr. Spittle had tied one through his buttonhole.

I believe Mrs. Spittle was even quieter, following this, and Ruth was so good with her. I never know what to say to a sad person—I usually just end up making them some tea; but there was none of that to be had, just now. My own shock at the suddenness of the death made *me* stare at the dead son's picture while I worked in grave silence. It haunted me to think that such a happy, robust face, which was once so *real*, just no longer existed in the world.

Mr. Spittle was far quieter even than Mrs. Spittle. I had been working on his farm for a month, and I had never heard him string more than five words together; even at mealtime conversation, and that was when he did his talking. From sunup, through the day's work, until the tractor and disk were put away, he never said a word. But from a few comments made by Mrs. Spittle, I do not think this was always the case. He was very kind to us girls—by manner (no words)—but I think he would have preferred that it be his own sons behind him, digging potatoes.

There were times when I would catch him staring out at his fields, or watching a robin wrestle an earthworm, and he would have a particular, pensive smile on his face so that I would not have been in the least surprised if he had burst out with a line of poetry. He never did. Invariably he would turn away, almost ashamed, and go on about his work with mindless busyness. He was a fascinating man...a puzzle. I never doubted that he could be downright inspiring if he gave it the least amount of effort.

My fellow soldiers in the Women's Land Army were a motley lot. Many of them were, like myself, from small countryside villages, but only three of them were from this particular village. The rest of us were far from home. A few were from the cities; Anne, our most recent addition, was from Manchester. She was still adjusting to gravel and poultry and outdoor plumbing. She had turned 17 three months before, was conscripted, and sent through the system to Mr. Spittle's farm. The government must have supposed he needed more help keeping up England's supply of potatoes. She was a good girl—a little hoity-toity, but she would soon work out of that, we all knew.

I was not conscripted, myself. I enlisted like any self-respecting eighteen-year-old Englishwoman. My mother served as a land girl in the Great War, and thoroughly enjoyed herself. I think she was honored to hear that her daughter would be serving the WLA, too—she was more honored than I was, actually. I have no qualms with digging potatoes, sheaving barley, and wringing chickens' necks when the need arises, but I would much rather do it at home.

But my family's farm is not relied upon to supply food for the nation in wartime; larger farms, like Mr. Spittle's, are. The farmers who run those farms ordinarily rely on their sons, and do not have them. So the government called upon the young women of England to form up their own troops, to fire on badgers that threaten innocent poultry communities and drive back weeds that have the nerve to compete for the potatoes' nutrients.

I have spent the time since my placement on Mr. Spittle's farm chronicling my sprawling thoughts about the matter onto every scrap sheet of paper that comes to me. By the way...

I wonder who is reading this, and when. Where did you find it? Were you snooping through my satchel? I hope not—it's full of my clean underwear, as you would know. I write this—well goodness, what is it?—a long journal entry—in the hopes that it will not be found, ever, or if it is, not until I am old and can honestly deny any recollection of it.

Perhaps you found it in the attic of my elderly granddaughter, in a trunk she keeps of my things and doesn't know why. Maybe you are a wee thing with an imagination as big as your heart, and far bigger than your experience. Or, maybe you are my great-grandson, the reprobate, who left his country roots to become a lawyer. Maybe you came across these yellowed papers and are getting a good laugh from them before you use them to kindle the bonfire that is to be the final resting place of your late mother's darling mementos, for which your corrupted heart has no purpose. Oh, bother...I think I am the young thing with an imagination far bigger than my brains.

Either way, be you snoopy soldieress, distant relative with heart of gold or iron, or a total stranger who is vowing to avoid my descendants because they will obviously have a delinquent streak, you are getting impatient with me. I am neglecting to say more about my odd episode in the potato fields. Well, you've got me. I was hoping you would forget. I see now that is not going to be possible. You just won't let me have peace about it.

But you see, I can't explain it, and the whole affair is more than a little disturbing. For it only got worse: as I was helping Mrs. Spittle dice potatoes for that evening's stew, she came across my...hmm...friend...in the sack of freshly dug potatoes. Her face wore the most expression I have seen on it since her son was K.I.A.—she was wholly disgusted that such a monster had been in with the other, more wholesome potatoes, and she gave it a pitch across the kitchen toward the scrap bucket. I caught it mid-air.

Both Mrs. Spittle and Ruth looked fairly shocked. I stammered out, "May I keep it?"

Mrs. Spittle blinked three times. "Why would you want it, dear?"

"I...I don't know," I confessed, in full honesty. "I'll probably feed it to the pigs, later on."

Mrs. Spittle nodded slowly, and the faint suggestion of astonishment faded from her face. She went back to mechanically dicing potatoes, a blank gaze fixed on her work. Ruth still watched me, highly concerned. I gave her a witless smile, dropped the stricken potato into my overalls pocket, and set back to work. I did not blame Ruth for worrying about me; I worried about me a great deal. Believe me, if you have never had the experience: the day you save a half-rotten potato from the scrap tin is a day of soul-searching.

Perhaps you are wondering what I did with the potato? I fed it to the pigs. Disappointed? Ha! If you are, then I hereby declare you unfit to judge me. You read of my rescuing a rotten potato with amusement, or even scorn, but you are disappointed at how it all turned out. You were secretly hoping something delightful would come out of it. Well, how do you know it did not? Perhaps I skipped a little. Maybe there were quite a lot of goings-on that elapsed between me saving the potato and gifting it to the swine. And now that we have established that you have no bragging rights over me, I can tell you about it.

(By the way, if you truly never doubted me, but always knew I had some good reason, then you knew more than I did and I love you. Stop by sometime, and I will make you a pot of tea, if you are sad.)

First things first: dinner. No silly whims of mine will ever keep me from attending to food. I finished cooking supper, and then, as you might suppose, I helped eat it. But after gleefully relinquishing the mound of dirty dishes to Ruth, I had opportunity to attend to my insanity. I am going to stop calling it that. How strange is it, really, to be fascinated by a unique potato (twice)? There are some who would say I am only observant, and appreciative of the small things in life. For fear of an alternative explanation I am going to agree with them… whoever they are.

And *there* is the original question: what was it about that potato that captured my attention? In order to think about it, I took me off to my cot in the loft of Mr. Spittle's barn, which he had kindly altered to be a remarkably comfortable place for us girls to live. Lying on my cot did not help me with the nagging question. So, I decided the only way to find out anything about my potato was to destroy it.

There were no convenient tools for said murder in the barn loft, so I went back to the kitchen and made ready with one of Mrs. Spittle's paring knives. Then I realized…I ought to do this methodically. Once cut, the potato couldn't very well be pasted together again, so I had to be *sure*. Should I cut the potato in half pole-to-pole, or across the equator? Then I thought, how very silly; a potato hasn't got poles and an equator like an orange has. So I just followed the cut Mr. Spittle's disk had left—at least, I started to.

My knife caught partway on something harder than one would expect from a potato. I pulled the knife out carefully, and tried to look down into the cut. It was not big enough to offer much of a view, so I took out another little wedge, just deep enough to uncover another piece of the hard thing. I held it up to the light, and the thing *shone back at me!*

I tell you, it is an odd thing to find a shiny something in a potato. I carved out a little more, gradually digging down to the object and trying not to scratch it. Whatever it was, I marveled that it had not been cut in two by the disk, which had sliced right down to it. Eventually, I pried it free. I could not believe it.

Grown into that potato was a *gold ring*.

There was no stone setting, and I thought it looked too broad to be a lady's ring. There were no engravings, that I could see, to identify it. This was a shocking turn of events. Perhaps I wasn't off my rocker after all—I was turning into a metal detector.

Most of the girls had already retired to the barn loft, and Mr. and Mrs. Spittle had escaped to their bench in the small cottage flower garden.

I hated to disturb them, but I thought they might want to know their potato crop was producing gold rings.

As I rounded the corner of the cottage, I stopped and watched them from a distance. They did not see or hear me. They both looked so quiet and sad that I began to doubt whether the situation was really all that urgent. I resolved to show it to Mrs. Spittle first thing in the morning, and I left them in peace.

All the others greeted me with snores as I creaked up the ladder. I cast around to be sure I was not being observed, and then I looped a handkerchief though the ring, tied it in a knot, and tucked it under my satchel (which is all I have for a pillow).

Now it happened that on this night my *dear* fellow land girls had a secret of their own.

It began with one of them finding a dead rat. She, being utterly un-squeamish, thought it funny and showed it to a few of the others. They were disgusted in the extreme, but all agreed it would be a jolly circus to hide it beneath some unlucky girl's pillow (as, after all, it would not be *their* pillow). Such obnoxious behavior was something one would think our captain, Marianne, would condemn; after all, bureaucratically speaking, we are an army, and order is paramount. This might have mattered if Marianne had not happened to be the one who found the rat.

After clandestine collusion, apparently it was decided that I was to be their hapless victim. Why they hated me with such a passion, I do not know.

Of course, when Marianne gathered her vicious gang at midnight and weaseled her hand under my pillow (I sleep like a hibernating badger), what should she find but a rather manly-looking handkerchief with a—*gasp*—gold ring tied on?

On went the oil lamps. The girls from No Man's Land—those who had neither been conscripted into Marianne's gang, nor witnessed my reckless intervention in a potato's demise—woke up looking more than a little confused. When I opened my own eyes, the first things I saw were the glassy eyes of a dead rodent dangling from Marianne's hand.

She was staring down at her other hand, which was holding my handkerchief, with ring still attached. The others finally saw what it was, took it from her, and passed it around, engaging in squealing and speculating and other general nuisancery.

"Look, it's a man's handkerchief," one observed.

Another surmised, "Maybe she's got a secret lover."

"I have *not*." I put that one down hard.

"Perhaps he died?" was sympathetically whispered by somebody.

"Yes, and she's too heartbroken to talk about him."

"No!" I cried, uselessly. "He never existed, so how could he have died?"

"Well, maybe it was her brother."

"Yes, and he's a soldier."

"Or maybe she inherited it."

"Or," said Marianne ominously, "maybe she *stole* it." She looked down on me with dark suspicion.

This was really too much. "What?" I shrieked. "*What?!*"

"Hush," cried Ruth, rushing over to my cot. "You'll wake Mr. Spittle, and then he'll be angry."

"Mr. Spittle, *angry?*" I retorted, still yelling. A few girls hid smiles, but not very well.

Marianne assumed a regal demeanor... somewhat spoiled by the rat. Brushing up her

Army Captain's vocabulary, she informed me, "I am confiscating these items until more can be ascertained." Ruth readied herself in case she be obliged to muffle my next outburst, but I did not make it necessary.

"So it's guilty until proven innocent, is it?" was all I muttered as Marianne ordered us all back to bed. She tossed the rat down the ladder and tucked my handkerchief and the Spittles' ring under her own pillow. (She had a *real* pillow.)

I was much too befuddled and besmirched to sleep anymore that night, so I watched Marianne sleep and struggled to keep down bitter thoughts. Maybe it was my pride that was hurt the most. What had I ever done to make them think I would steal a gold ring? Any of the other girls' absurd notions made more sense than that one. Marianne must have been crazier than I was.

But I had better cut to the marrow of this account before I bring on a paper ration.

When I awoke, the other girls were still asleep—except Marianne. She was nowhere to be seen, so I crept over to her cot and moved her pillow to see if she had already removed the suspicious items. She had, naturally. I pulled on my overalls and flew down the ladder, to find

Marianne strolling across the drive-in to where Mrs. Spittle sat with her flowers.

My heart stuttered, but my feet did not. In an instant I thought of what might happen if Marianne told the Spittles I had stolen the ring, and if they believed her. The thought that Marianne had no proof to back her accusations never crossed my mind.

I did hesitate a moment—what if Marianne was going to speak to Mrs. Spittle about something else entirely?

In that moment, Marianne pulled my handkerchief out of her pocket and dashed that idea. I started running again. I thought of calling out, "Thank you, Marianne! You found my handkerchief!" or some other such nonsense, but that would only make me look more suspicious as soon as Marianne started talking.

So I decided not to give her a chance.

I stopped running a few paces away and walked calmly up. In Marianne's surprise, I was able to quietly take the "items" out of her hand. By the time she snapped to, I was already explaining to Mrs. Spittle what had happened. I told her of the potato, and how I had decided to figure out why it fascinated me so, and how I cut it open and found the ring.

When I said "ring," she looked puzzled. I unclenched my grip on the wadded handkerchief and untied it. I handed her the ring. "I assumed it must belong to you and Mr. Spittle, and I was waiting till morning to bring it to you."

She took the ring from my fingertips with wonder. After a few seconds, Mrs. Spittle looked at me and exclaimed, "You say you found this grown into a potato?"

I could not help but laugh at the absurdity of it all. In all of the emotions I had felt on account of this potato, I had not yet thought to laugh. "Yes, ma'am. I think that's why the potato was so rotten and deformed."

A gentle smile appeared on Mrs. Spittle's face, and she leaned close, as if to share a secret. "This was my son's," she said softly. "His college ring. He went away to get his education, but he came back to us, to work the farm. That's why it was always so dear to me, to see it on his finger… it made me thankful that my son was made of better gold than a grand university could offer him. See, he worked so hard in it, he wore the engravings off." She pointed to the widening at the top of the ring, where an imprint must have once been.

She slowly nodded. "I think he wore it down on purpose. He wanted it bare. He always used to say that gold should not have to be gilded. It bothered him that people think it must be engraved and beautified. He lost this ring planting seed potatoes last spring—the very crop you girls just brought in. He was very sad it was lost, and so was I." She stared at the ring for a moment, then she turned to me with a furrow in her brow. "But however did you know it was in that potato?"

"I didn't. I thought I was going mad."

Then Mrs. Spittle let out the first laugh I had ever heard from her lips. It was beautiful. "Well dear, if you are mad, don't you ever get your senses!"

Marianne had been listening to us talk with her jaw flapping, but Mrs. Spittle remembered her now. "I'm sorry—what was it that you needed, dear?"

Marianne shook her head and walked back to the barn, looking very, very confused.

I excused myself and left, but I looked back as I went. It was not much of a discovery, as you, finder of this account, may be accustomed to reading about in stories. But I daresay it brought more delight to Mrs. Spittle to see that ring again than a chest-full of gold would have done. I could not stop smiling at the picture of Mrs. Spittle cradling her son's ring in her hand, and often I have thanked the Lord for showing me that blessed potato.

A few day after this, I was again helping Mrs. Spittle in the kitchen, and I noticed that the ring had found a new home, tied to the identification tags of her fallen boy. But Mrs. Spittle no longer stared at the portraits forlornly. She was much more cheery in the kitchen, and even hummed from time to time. I think the return of some fond memories had done her good.

I know it was not I who brought the situation about. The Maker of that potato made the other girls leave it for me to find—and made me so very drawn to it, that I could not help but wonder why. I think I have learned something from it, too—reader, pardon me while I preach.

The exterior of that potato was rotten and decaying fast, and yet it held a priceless treasure—much as our decaying earthly bodies may hide the gold of eternal things. One would never have guessed the potato held treasure, to look only on its outside. I certainly did not. So it is with people. Mrs. Spittle seemed to be not much more than a quiet presence before, but a mere bit of comforting sentiment in her grieving brought back the real Mrs. Spittle. Mr. Spittle, too, underwent a similar change (to a far less drastic degree) when Mrs. Spittle showed him the ring. And—I am not sure—but I think and even hope that it may yet prove true for Marianne.

Furthermore, the gold hidden in the potato had something to do with the potato's troubles. On account of the gold, it could not grow right, so it was despised and rejected. But its temporary trials only made the discovery more sweet when the decay was cut away at last and its treasure made plain.

There it is, great-great-granddaughter/ heartless great-grandson/stranger; do with my ramblings as you will. I have said my piece. Now that we have all decided that perhaps I am not about to join the march hares after all, I think I must get back to planting seed potatoes. I wonder what treasures we will discover next harvest, in such precious potatoes as these.

THE THING IS

Answer the Bell
When It Calls

Dear Eamonn,

You ask very interesting questions. I thoroughly enjoyed reading the ones in your letter, and I even had to laugh at the priceless innocence of a few of them. If that makes no sense to you now, perhaps it will someday. Too few people at my stage of living ask such innocent questions—more's the pity.

It occurred to me, at the end, that indeed you would expect me to answer your questions. I only hope I can answer them as interestingly as you delivered them. I don't expect I can, but here's a go.

Firstly, you asked if I knew how much the great bell weighs. I have never undertaken to weigh it, myself; in fact, I do not imagine it has been weighed since it was cast (and on account of a fire in the town's record hall fifty-two years ago, no one knows for certain when that was). But I have been told—and agree—that one would not want to be in its shadow if ever that headstock should break and the bell return to earth.

It has happened more than once, I hear: the positively ancient ropes that held up the bell frayed away and dropped it. I am told that the most recent incident was in 1723, though we cannot be sure (unfortunate, that records fire). The story goes that it fell in the dead of night, and the locals went fleeing to the hills, afraid that the priest had finally gone batty (apparently there was some preexisting concern). Local ears did not stop ringing for four days afterward, so the old ones used to say—not that they were around. The seven-meter fall to the stone floor of the bell tower did not crack the brass—which is a wonder, because it was (allegedly) a frigid winter—but it did squish it some. The bell is a whole centimeter shorter than it used to be, it is thought. But again, we cannot be certain. I am sure at this point I need not explain why.

I confess, some days I take a good long look at those "new" ropes before I ring the bell. After all, those ropes that lash the bell to the headstock are 209 years old, and by my reckoning, they are due for another fall. As the bell ringer, I imagine I am the most at risk for being mashed. If I ever see fraying, I will retire.

All right now…this is my fault, I realize. I was laughing too hard to correct you when you first mentioned it, but I've got control of me now. The dancing alpacas you saw engraved around the crown of the bell are not alpacas at all. Humans, they are, lad. Humans. The bell-founder was, reportedly, a man fond of feasting, and so that is what he portrayed the Saints doing. What about it made you think of *alpacas*? I couldn't be sure I know what those are, but they are not anything on the bell. I know that.

You remember the bell tower, don't you? I wish you could have seen it up close, but your father was right to warn you about climbing up to it. The breakers make those rocks down below look craggier every year, and I can only manage to make the pass myself by studiously not thinking about the twenty-meter fall I would take to land on them.

I am glad monastic rule is a thing of the past...any institution that produces monks who will design the pathway from the church to the bell tower to run mere centimeters from the precipice is not something I want ruling over me. Perhaps I am speaking unjustly—it is entirely possible that the cliff has eroded quite a bit since the 14th century. In those days, the path may have been a safe distance from the cliff. Twenty years ago, the margin between the path and the cliff edge was 15 centimeters wide. Now it is 14½. If I live to see it drop to 13, I will retire.

It is a very large bell tower, for an ancient church on a coastal island, and it conveniently has a small room attached to the side of it; which, I think, must have served as a recorder's room in times long past. I think I told you before: that little room is where I live. Yes, now I remember, I did...you were amazed that I lived in so small a place, and were worried that I got lonely. I assured you that I do not, and introduced you to my rook friend, Lorcan. Remember? By the way, Lorcan sends his greetings. I think you caught his fancy (it may have had something to do with the sweet bread you gave him).

I am neglecting your questions. Let me see…ah, yes, you wondered why you did not see anyone but me at the church. Eamonn, it is because there are only seven people left in this little village. When the church structure was built some half a millenium ago, a goodly community sprang up around it, but the many subsequent generations have lost a few members here and there until we have dwindled down to the way we are now. I don't believe our village was ever large, but the Industrial Revolution delivered its death blow. Everyone who could do so uprooted and joined the rest of the nation in searching for work and food on the mainland, and here we find ourselves now: seven souls, and all of us graying at the temples.

We all came to terms long ago with the fact that our village will soon be gone, and we have determined to live out its declining years in peace. I still ring the bell on the hour, and all seven of us gather in the moss-covered church ruins every Lord's Day. We know that it will not be long until only six gather. Then five, then four, and finally there will only be one of us, and we have all made a pact that the one left standing will ring the bell, pull the tall weeds around the headstones, and tend (and eat) the sheep. We are all at peace with our plan.

Even yet, it stirs a bit of hope that perhaps it will not have to be that way when young things like you and your parents (you may think them old, but they are very young) come and pay us a visit. Quite honestly, we thought the rest of the island—let alone the rest of Ireland—had clean forgotten about us. Your brief sojourn in our hole in the world was the highlight of our year...the highlight of our last five years.

So you see, I was only teasing when I said I would retire should the cliff pass fall away, or the ropes drop the bell on me. (Well, I guess I might have to retire, then.) I would stay, and I would fix them, because if I am the last bellringer in a string of 500 years of bellringers, what kind of man would I be if I gave up? I shall stick with it, and die in my bell tower. I hope. I may die by falling on the rocks at the cliff foot, but I would rather die in the bell tower. Seems a tad more dignified.

My land, what morbid things for me to be writing to an eleven-year-old lad! Forgive me. I will answer your question about the bell rope, now. Do you know you are very methodical? You asked about the bell, and then you moved in a logical manner down to the bell rope. A sense of method is a good trait in a bellringer...I'm only saying.

The bell rope is not nearly as old as the church, or even the bell. I can tell you with certainty that the current bell rope is forty-six years old, and really ought to be replaced. I know, because I braided it myself as soon as I took the job of bellringer. Took me two months. It is tradition—in this village, at least—for the bellringers to make the bell ropes. I suppose that is logical, too; what do you think?

You said, when you were looking over from the churchyard, that you thought you saw a plaque in the floor of the bell tower. You did. It is as old as the bell tower, and informs us that it was completed in 1400. You may wonder why, then, we don't know when the bell was hung, but stories roam that it was many years before the bell—though commissioned around the same time the tower was being finished—actually arrived. There are tales of it almost being lost to sea, and other such excuses.

Now for your more discomfiting question... How did I come to be the bellringer of a medieval church on an island? You took me aback with that one, lad. I hope sincerely that you are asking because you wish to enter the noble profession yourself. (You would have to throw all your weight into it, but pretend the rope is a swing and I think you could pull it just fine.) But I hope just as strongly that you do not go about it the way I did. I was a year older than you when I took up the task.

I found it available because, when I stumbled upon it, the old bellringer had just died. His heart failed him when he was going to ring four o'clock. He missed the fourth ring, and the locals went about their day as if it were three o'clock and wondered how it came to be dark so early. It is not at all funny, but I thought it was, then. But that is the most minor way in which I did wrong.

I have been told that I was born on this island. Of course, I am dependent on my parents' recollection; I don't remember a thing of the event. More specifically, I was born (allegedly) on one among a smattering of farms on the side of the island that faces the mainland.

I was quite a wild lad. This I remember for myself. When I turned twelve, my father tried to rein me in by giving me the heavy responsibility of minding his cattle, and I kicked. I revolted. Every untried plan that had been swimming in my brash head was screaming against this new restraint, one that to me seemed everlasting—and then there was also the pressing matter of my higher education, which my mother would never let me forget. My father would not relent on either score; he was determined to make a man of me yet.

So I ran. I escaped one night and put as much distance as I could between me and my father's farm. I traveled clear to the opposite side of the island in one night, with nothing to my name but the feet that carried me.

Having reached the cliff edge and the sea, I was not going any further. Just before dawn, I collapsed in the cemetery of this church, where the parson found me in the early morning on his way to his study. He brought me home with him and gave me breakfast, and very kindly demanded to know where I was from and how I came to be sleeping in his graveyard.

I am afraid I cried—I was only twelve, after all, and I was beginning to regret my rash revolt. I remember the parson's eyebrows, working like ocean waves as I spilled my soul on him. Looking back, I think he used them to distract me from his mouth, which must have been badly tempted to laugh at my pitiful state.

As much as I was already beginning to miss my father's heavy hand and my mother's cottage pie, my pride was still stiff enough to keep me from turning my face toward home. The parson allowed me stay on the church grounds, but I was to work as long as I boarded there.

He showed me the bell, gave me a reliable old pocket watch, and told me I was to ring the bell for the hours. And for the sake of all that ran smoothly, I was not to botch it up. He did not present it so terribly, but the prospect of what might ensue if I did fumble with the time was enough to keep me in line. His wife made me a gift of a blanket and pillow, and in the tiny tower side-room I lived. I ate from the parson's own table, in exchange for clearing tall weeds from around the headstones when they sprang up, and doing other similar gardening work at the church. I drank up my newfound freedom.

But it lasted, undisturbed, for only four days. My distraught father had been searching the island over. He was running out of places to hunt for me, and he feared I had left the island entirely. Then he rode into this village (what there was of it) one afternoon, and whom should he meet there but the parson?

Of course, the parson knew exactly who my father was looking for. He sat my father down on a big, flat headstone in the cemetery, then he led me to him and left us to battle it out. I have been grateful that he did so ever since.

Father ranted and wept and hugged me and cuffed me upside the head by turns. The round ended with me holding him as tight as I could and sobbing into his armpit. When I was through snuffling my remorse, he sat me back down and asked what I had been doing all this time.

When I confessed that I had been living in a 480-year-old, 3-square-meter stone room and ringing the church bell on the hour (and enjoying myself immensely), he laughed. Oh, I will never forget that laugh. He laughed and laughed and laughed and then he cried. I think he was only glad that I had run away to work for a clergyman by the sea, rather than a tavern-keeper in Dublin, as my older brother had elected to do. We talked over some particulars, and later that evening he left me at the church, promising to bring my mother and sisters to see me at work as soon as lambing was over.

Here I have lived ever since. The parson and his wife had no children, and I was offered their cottage thirty years ago, when they passed. But I turned it down. I had long before built a fireplace into the tower room and furnished it with a fold-away bed. Having been granted a salary, I could provide food for myself. I spent my evenings and wet days reading every book that came within a mile of me. (For all my disdain for school, reading was and is my life's blood.) I could not imagine how another home could possibly be more suited for me.

Eamonn, I do hope you become a bellringer, even if you do not wish to live in such quarters as I do. It is not the sort of glamorous occupation the young bucks are after these days, but it is satisfying. But go about it rightly. Don't leave your father's cattle alone to wander themselves off a cliff in the night.

Are you satisfied, then? I have done my best to answer many of your questions, but I have had to leave the most innocent and important alone—regrettably.

Michael (the oldest of us seven) rides our mail out to the nearest town with a postal service, and he weighs every piece. Envelopes are flatly refused if they weigh more than an ounce. None of the other six of us like this arbitrary stipulation of his, but he is our only way of contacting the outside world, and so we go along. I cannot send any more with this letter; I already fear an envelope and stamp will be the straw that breaks Michael's back. Perhaps there will be a sequel.

Greet your mother for me, and tell her I found a large clump of gorse near the church the other day. I shall dig some up for her to take home if ever your family visits again. Is it true that gorse does not grow in your dandy cities? I say that is another reason I shall bide my days in this forgotten corner. I could not do without my lovely gorse.

Greet your father, too, if you please. Tell him I have begun to comb the records (those that are left) for any mention of his great-great-grandfather (do I have that right?), but I have found nothing as of yet. I will keep diligently at it, though, until I upturn something.

You may also tell him that I look forward to arguing over sheep breeds with him again. If he ever finds his wool trade slacking in that city of yours, you tell him there is plenty of wool here; only, no people to sell it to. You bring the people, and we will give 'em sheep. And I'll throw in the most beautiful bell tones this side of Limerick.

And as for you…take care, lad.
Hoping the bell continues to call you,

— Innis O'Callaghan

THE THING IS

Pipes & Strings

My story begins, as I suppose many do, with a fog. It was not any dramatic fog, though. Not a "pea-soup-er," as some say. A halfhearted fog, it may be thought, is not the most thrilling setting for the beginning of a story. But I cannot help that; a halfhearted fog it was, and I shall be truthful.

The side streets of Daren-Felyn were as empty as my head that morning, and very cold. (For indeed, whoever heard of a warm fog?) Now you should not think that I mean that I was empty-headed in the way you may be thinking of—the shallow type of person who deflates if the hot-air pump goes out. Such a person has no depth or interest at all unless they are puffing wind (hardly then). No…I do not think I could be accused of that, even if I say it myself.

I only mean that I had nothing in particular to think about that morning, just as the street had no one to walk on it. A journeyman does not often get to see a town at rest, for he is never at rest himself. I was enjoying this rare good look at life with roots. For myself, the mornings on which I have nothing in particular to think about are the cheerfullest, because that means there is nothing awfully disturbing afoot, and therefore it is easy to continually be in the sort of good mood that stops to listen to birdsong.

It was odd for a bird to be out warbling on a cold, halfway-foggy morning such as that one, when the clever people and the calendars tell us it is spring but we all know it isn't. But there was a bird out singing. It was none of my business if a bird had missed his southern flight, or come home early, so I sang along—which was very difficult. Have you ever tried to sing along with a bird? When you do not know the bird, you don't very well know their song. I am a journeyman, and the son of a journeyman. I did my growing up always shifting from one Welsh hill to the other dell, and nowhere had I ever heard a bird like this one. I gave up trying to mimic the bird and hummed an improvisation. We made pretty good harmony…to my ears, at least. The bird may have disagreed. Either way, I was in downright airy spirits and I had to work to keep myself from skipping my merry way down a public street.

But I was also very cold, so I did walk a little faster when I saw the wooden shingle over the shop which meant that warmth was near:

G.M. Cadwalader
Luthier & Fine Woodworker

Some cat protested when I opened the door. Her tail must have been trailing on the floor, and the door passed over it when I pushed through. Apparently this caused some kind of discomfort to the cat. Upon my word, I tried to apologize, but to this day, I do not think I am forgiven.

Her master was more pleased to see me. Coming from the back room of the shop, I heard a warm, "Good morning! Is that you, Mr. Maddox?" In a tick the man had appeared, confirmed that I was in fact Mr. Maddox, and clutched my right hand with both of his. I noted to myself that this Mr. Cadwalader was one of those men who make you feel as if shaking your hand is an honor they truly appreciate. I do not meet many such men in my line of work.

"Come this way, my good fellow." He beckoned me with a rheumatic finger and led me through to the back. I noticed that he had turned on his heel pretty stiffly. This drew my attention to the fact that his left leg was rigid, as if he did not have a knee.

When we popped out of the narrow confines of the hallway into his square workroom, he turned around and saw my eye upon his leg. Then I noticed his noticing, and from the temperature of my cheeks I think I turned very red. I was acting like a lad, staring like that! How could I?

Mr. Cadwalader smiled. "Oh yes, this leg of mine—it is a trouble. Do you know, I have never intentionally bent that knee in my life?" I tried to appear politely curious, and not as stupid as I felt. "I came from my mother's womb with a leg that don't work, and no doctors have ever been able to explain what ails it. It's simply limp. I have only ever managed to walk with it braced up stiff, like you see it now." He slapped his thigh and chuckled when his wedding ring *chinked* against something metal, even through his trousers.

He pushed his spectacles further up the bridge of his nose. "My father was killed in the Crimean War, a month before the war was over, and three weeks before I made my appearance in the world. Now you see, he'd been wounded in the knee a month or two before he was killed. They say he could only walk those last few weeks with a brace on the leg." Mr. Cadwalader peered mysteriously over his spectacles. "When I came to be born with the same trouble, the old wives about town told my mother that by dying before I could be born, my father had passed his injury to me."

I didn't know what kind of answer he expected. Apparently none. He cracked a huge smile and laughed. "Whatever sense *that* was supposed to make, I don't know." He had a way of kindly putting you at ease, and I could see now that he was trying to use this power on me.

He called me over to the back wall of the workroom. Only now I noticed that the room was an awful shambles. There was a bookshelf (with no books) moved away from the wall, and a great pile of wood, loose papers, and assorted tools on the worktable. He would have no room to work there, and judging from the immaculate neatness of the showroom I had seen out front, I deduced that this mingle-mangle was not the normal state of his workroom.

"You'll find the culprit in there somewhere, I expect," he said bitterly, and jabbed his knobbly finger towards a place where the plaster ceiling had fallen away. Below this, the old-fashioned, quintessentially Victorian wallpaper was water stained from top to bottom. The stain culminated in a sodden pile of sheets and blankets on the floor against the baseboard.

"You have the water turned off, sir?" I asked. (I have had my share of *oopses* in my work. You learn to double-check.) I set my toolbox on the floor by the pile of sheets and was about to set to inspecting the hole in the ceiling, to see if I could locate the trouble.

"Oh yes, water's off." Mr. Cadwalader walked slowly to his worktable and put his hands on the pile of wood there. He moaned. "That blasted leak—the pipe burst night before last, but neither my wife or I came in here till next morning to know about it. Oh, just see what it had done, Mr. Maddox! It ruined half of my best tonewoods."

I looked up to see him dolefully examining a highly flamed block of maple, about a foot long and three inches broad. The block was swollen and splintery all along one side. He looked at me, and I would not have been surprised if I had seen tears in his eyes. Shaking his head, he began shifting things on his work table. "I was eager to set to work with this maple. Would have made the prettiest fiddle neck your eyes ever saw. And this—" he held up a wide, thin spruce board, also warped and splitting. "This would have been a fiddle belly as would have truly *sang*." He shook his head again. "Absolutely ruined."

I pried away a chunk of plaster to expose more of the troublesome pipe in the ceiling. Quite a bit of the stuff fell to the floor. I knelt to pick it up and found a wee piece of perfectly black wood in a crack of the floorboards. It could not have been much more than a inch long. Surely this had to be a scrap. He had enough tidying up to do; I would throw it away for him. "Where's your wastebasket, Mr. Cadwalader?" I asked.

"Here it—" He turned to hand the basket to me and his eyes shot wide as a Welsh poppy. "Oh, that's not rubbish, Mr. Maddox! No! That's a nut I spent an hour shaping last Saturday. Hardest ebony I have ever worked. It was bound to be arguably the best nut I've ever made." He put a hand to his forehead. "Then I dropped it. All the sweeping I could do wouldn't make it turn up. But you've found it—" He smiled, relieved (and nervous, thinking about its near shave with the wastebasket) and quickly took the wee black thing out of my ignorant hands. "No, we'll not be throwing that away, sir!"

A *nut*…well then. I would not be touching any more scraps of wood on the floor; no sir. The pipe in the ceiling was now exposed enough that I could get to the problem, so I started to it. But I watched my client with a corner of my eye.

Mr. Cadwalader glumly moved pieces of wood and tools around on his worktable, to no purpose. After a few minutes he gave up and sat on his stool, with the foot of his stiff leg propped on the supports of the worktable.

There were three fiddles on the wall. He took down the middle one and sat with his hand gently wrapped around its willowy neck (or would that be a maple-y neck?) He took his time picking out a bow from the thirty he must have had hanging on nails over his worktable. Then he put the two together.

I realized it was not any birdsong I had been hearing on my walk that morning.

I have heard a smattering of fiddlers in my time. Some make you want to square up and shoot the owl. Some sound as if they are the very voice of the blood that runs in our Christian Celtic veins—strong in the joy of the Lord, never afraid to die if there's a good reason, and determined to be lively until then. The songs they play are wild, fast, with lots to say—especially when that fiddler digs into two strings at once. To some, I dance. To some, I listen, and my blood agrees with what it hears.

Mr. Cadwalader was different. Indeed—I had thought his playing was birdsong, and that should tell you something of its quality. If other fiddlers' fingers look like they are sashaying a reel, Mr. Cadwalader's fingers danced a minuet. One moment, they played near the fiddlehead, then they slipped up closer to Mr. Cadwalader and played higher notes, but no less pleasant ones. His bow clipped lightly across the strings. Now it stopped and dug in to make its point, but about the time you saw what it was doing, it was off again. Like a sprite. Or a wood-elf. Something like that.

Some players look focused. Mr. Cadwalader looked careless—but his music did not sound it. He was master, and the fiddle was his valued servant. He confidently told it what to do; the fiddle obeyed, and looked better in my eyes for having done it.

After a minute, he finished his song. He raised an eyebrow at me over his spectacles and smiled. I blinked and realized that I had completely stopped working.

—

When I stepped out of Mr. Cadwalader's shop a hour later, Daren-Felyn was no longer asleep, and I no longer had nothing to think about. I walked down the sidewalk with my head down. I felt heavy, but I did not know why. The people of the town were all on their important missions of the day. I stood on the corner where the side street to Mr. Cadwalader's shop met with the town's main thoroughfare and watched them all go.

The butcher's young son was carting off a ham wrapped in parchment—delivering it to some matron's larder, no doubt. It was half as big as he was, poor lad. There was the eggler, up and about, too. Three capped heads of households trumped past me, hobnail boots rattling on the cobbles, probably on their way to work at the quarry a mile outside town. I had walked past the quarries on my way into town two days ago. Three doors behind me, a girl tripped up to someone's front door carrying a crock wrapped in a towel. The delightful lass told the old woman who came to the door that she had brought some beef broth, and hoped the woman's cold wouldn't keep her from church on Sunday. Then she was off on her way back down the street.

I envied these people. They got to live in this town with a man like Mr. Cadwalader.

I had almost skipped down the street at dawn. Now I plodded my way the other direction, doing figures in my head to decide how long I could afford to stay in Daren-Felyn before I must uproot and move on to see what plumbers' laments the next village was suffering from.

What happened to me?

I jerked my hands out of my pockets. None of that. I slid my cap's brim high up my forehead so that my eyes were open to the world. I opened them a little wider. I had woken up in a good mood that morning, but I was letting myself slip back into my customary pragmatic slump. Too much like another man I knew...I might have his eyes, nose, and occupation, but I did not want his life. I remember commenting to myself, when I was about ten, that my father's head was never turned. I gradually noticed, through experience, that this meant there were some good things he never saw.

I looked over my shoulder. The mid-morning sun, mild as it was, had burned off most of the fog, and even from here I could make out Mr. G.M. Cadwalader's shop sign far down the street behind me. I *had* seen something beautiful this morning, and I was not going to be fool enough to act like I hadn't. I spun sharply on my heel like I had seen Mr. Cadwalader do and marched straight back to that good man's door.

"Mr. Cadwalader, sir?" I peered in. The room had only one tiny transom window high on the street-side wall, so it was a dark place. Just now, as I was standing with the door open, a wedge of sunlight shouldered in around me, so I could barely see anything. I blinked to adjust my eyes and looked into the corners of the room. The cat was nowhere in sight. Neither was Mr. Cadwalader.

A clock was ticking. Now the cat let me know that she *was* in fact here, by hissing at me from behind a stack of violin cases in the corner. They looked like coffins. The cat slunk out and sat down defiantly in front me, right where my head was casting a shadow on the floorboards. Smooth floorboards, but wavy, with paths worn into them by a century or two of tin-soled boots like the ones I was wearing. I pushed the door open all the way and was in the shop. The bell called out to tell its master that somebody was here. A little over-cheery, it was. I had not noticed it this morning.

What was I doing here? I had work I needed to get to…somewhere. Surely somebody else in this town had a busted pipe they would gladly pay me to fix. I ran my eyes over the half-dozen fiddles hanging in the shop. Or a leaky drain, maybe. I turned around to go. Then I saw the fiddle lying on the counter.

I leaned to glance through the door at the back of the room. No sign of Mr. Cadwalader. Maybe he had not heard the bell. I took one step closer to the counter. Why was I tip-toeing? I don't know.

The fiddle was like a fine lady, and I felt for all the world like a stableboy who knows very well that he does not belong in the same room with her. You might admire what a picture such a lady made, for looking at, but to touch even the brim of her hat would be…well, you just wouldn't do it. There are just some things you expect to go your entire life only looking at from afar. The fiddles I saw in Mr. Cadwalader's shop fell in that category—especially the one lying so fetchingly on the counter in front of me.

The wood was so thin. How did *anybody* touch it? The varnish was just the color of black tea. It was dark and mellow at the flourishing edge, and just a bit more blonde on the high belly. The curves and points of the sides…the perfect scrolling of the fiddle-head…the orderly winding of the strings on the pegs…how on earth do strings so dainty sing so powerfully? There were scratches and scars on the wood, and variations in the varnish. But—not in spite of these things—one looked at that violin and thought, *perfect*.

I thought of how Mr. Cadwalader had looked that morning as he played. He was obviously a craftsman worthy of using such an instrument. I was not. I was glad Mr. Cadwalader was not in the room, so that I might just stand beside that instrument and marvel at it in secret.

Of course, Mr. Cadwalader chose this very moment to come downstairs. "Coming! Sorry to keep you waiting," I heard him call from the stairs. "I was helping my wife lay out breakfast when I heard the bell ring." He switched on the light and popped through the door. He looked from me, to the violin on the counter, and back again. "Ah, Mr. Maddox. What brings you back?"

I coughed. *See?* I lectured myself. *Even Mr. Cadwalader thinks you have work you ought to be at.* But I did need to account for myself somehow, now. "Your playing, sir. It was…it was fascinating. That's all, sir. I'm sorry I troubled you to come down from breakfast. I'll be off now." However much my feet wanted out of that room, my boots did not want to go. I looked down again at the violin on the counter.

For some reason I will never know, I kept talking. "Truthfully, sir, I've never seen a violin up close before."

Mr. Cadwalader snorted. "Fiddles, I prefer to call them. We're no Frenchies here." But then he looked at me with wonder and smiled. "But is that so, Mr. Maddox? You have never seen one?"

"Well…not like this, sir. I've heard lots of 'em played, but never really *noticed* them before, if you understand me. This one is…so pretty."

Mr. Cadwalader laughed kindly. "And it's got you under its spell. Say no more; I understand more than you know." He picked up the fiddle from the counter. "Well then, you should try it."

"Try what?"

"The fiddle, lad."

How my eyes must have bugged! "Oh, no sir. I've taken up too much of your time already. I'm not the kind to, to, well, you know—" I gestured pathetically at the fiddle and turned around to go (flee, that is).

Mr. Cadwalader raised an eyebrow. "Nonsense. Hold it," he ordered.

Chastened, I turned back around. He pushed the fiddle toward me. I took it my hands, but they hardly knew what to hold. The fiddle did not weigh anything. I felt like I did when my mother laid my infant sister in my arms for the first time, years and years ago. "Won't it break?" I whispered to Mr. Cadwalader in mild terror.

His smile belied his amusement. "Yes, I suppose it could, but it's sturdier than you give it credit for." He looked at me pointedly over the rim of his spectacles. "Why are you afraid of it?"

Afraid of a fiddle? Ridiculous! But yes.

Mr. Cadwalader reached over the counter and flipped the fiddle over in my hands. "Just look at that, Mr. Maddox!" He beamed and waited for me to react appropriately. It was a lovely sight, I agreed. "It's a one-piece back, you see. Most fiddle-backs are in two pieces." He pulled a second fiddle off the wall for me to compare. Then he pointed at the one in my hand. "I did not build that one, you see. I only fixed it up. It's an old girl." He looked up at the ceiling and counted under his breath. "Eleventy years old, now," he declared with a wink.

I smiled. I was getting *slightly* more comfortable with the fiddle being in my hands. I moved it to let the light move over its back. "Those dark lines in the grain—is that naturally in the wood?" I asked. "Looks like it was drawn there with a pencil, almost."

"That is called spalting. Most interesting, isn't it?" Mr. Cadwalader gazed fondly at the fiddle. "Oh yes, it's naturally in the wood. Just think, Mr. Maddox: until a luthier planed and scraped out that fiddle-back from a tree trunk, no living eyes had ever seen that pattern. If a timber-cutter had not chosen that tree, we'd have never seen it at all. But the grain pattern, the spalting, the loveliness, would still have served its entire purpose. It would have been no waste. It would have pleased God." He looked at me seriously. "We should count ourselves blessed that He shared the enjoyment with us."

I looked at the fiddle with even more wonder.

Mr. Cadwalader's eyes twinkled at me. "Remember, Mr. Maddox: it's a box of wood. Nothing more. An incredibly detailed, delicate, *singing* box of wood, but still—only that." He pointed at my chest. "But you are a man. Made in your Maker's image. Given dominion over all Creation, including music. You are master—" now he pointed at the fiddle in my hands—"and this is a tool, at your disposal. It waits for you to command it."

He crossed the room and picked out a bow from the rack on the wall. "That does not guarantee you will play well, Mr. Maddox," he chuckled. "Every good master knows his own limitations, and makes use of the talents of those under his authority." He tapped the shoulder of the fiddle and nodded sagely. "This is a lovely instrument, and that's reason to respect it. But don't *fear* it, my boy." He handed me the chosen bow. "Take dominion, Mr. Maddox."

My shoulders relaxed. Relenting, I laughed. I looked down at the fiddle in my one hand, and the bow in my other. "You're going to have to show me how."

—

I scraped out a handful of sorry notes that day, with Mr. Cadwalader leading my hands and roundly praising every minuscule improvement (and minuscule they were—believe me). I trotted off down the street that afternoon with a broad smile on my face. The memory of it still makes my cheeks sore.

Back I came the next morning before work, as I had been commanded, for Mr. Cadwalader to guide me through playing a few more notes ever so *slightly* less ear-gutting. So it went for a week...

Until the morning I had to tell Mr. Cadwalader that I would have to pack up. I had exhausted the plumbing work in Daren-Felyn, I explained, and my pockets kept giving me hints—decreasingly subtle—that I needed to move on. I reflected, only to myself, that I might never again have the chance to hold a fiddle. I shook Mr. Cadwalader's hand and thanked him as warmly as I could for what he had given me.

Mr. Cadwalader's forehead furrowed deeper and deeper as I talked. "Oh dear...oh dear," he muttered over and again. "Can't have that.

No." He ordered me to stay right where I was standing for the moment.

Coming around the edge of the counter with agility one does not expect from a man with a stiff leg, he went to the corner of the shop and pulled a violin case out of the row. He grabbed up a bow from the wall on his way back behind the counter. He plopped down the case, flipped open the lid, and nestled the black-tea colored fiddle in its hollow. The bow was deftly slipped into its place in the lid. A cake of rosin wrapped in flannel was tucked snuggly by the fiddlehead. Mr. Cadwalader fastened down the latches of the case and double-checked each one. Then he took it all up and held it out to me.

Surely not. "What are you doing, sir?" I breathed.

Mr. Cadwalader smiled. I looked at him carefully. His eyes were misty behind his spectacles. "I'm trusting that you won't hurt an old man's heart—that you'll love this fiddle well, and for as long as you can."

That was now twenty years ago. It took some doing, truly, but eventually Mr. Cadwalader persuaded me to accept his gift. He even thought to re-fit the case with a shoulder strap of thick leather to make it easier for me to carry on my travels. I walked out of Daren-Felyn that afternoon possessing a fiddle, and a friend.

Most evenings, I sit down in the square of whatever town I am in, and play for the birds—and for any people who care to listen. I am no Mr. Cadwalader, but I am a better player than I used to be. And every evening, I am watching. I am waiting to see some young soul in the shadows of the twilight, eyes wide with wondering at the singing box in my hands, surprised by the yearning they feel. I will be glad to help them understand it.

If this book tickled your noggin

and you find yourself feeling a tad

nosey about other available titles

and forthcoming releases, visit

nogginnose.com

NOGGINNOSE

PRESS

a curious name for curiouser books